Dawson's Down!

A STORY OF SACRIFICE

By DON PATTERSON

Illustrated by Sonny Schug

Dawson's Down!
By Don Patterson
Illustrated by Sonny Schug/Studio West
Edited by Mary Parenteau
Production by Kline/Phoenix Advertising Graphics

© 2000, 2010 Hindsight Limited

Published in Minneapolis, MN by Rising Star Studios, LLC.

Picture Credits
Many thanks to the following organizations for giving permission to reprint illustrations and text used in the "In Hindsight" section of this book.
Special thanks to Ian Huntley for research and text.
p. 93 Courtesy Ian Huntley, Aerocam
p. 95 Seaplanes of the World, O.G. Publishing, 1997
p. 96 Courtesy Ian Huntley, Aerocam

Printed in China:
Shenzhen Donnelley Printing Co., Ltd
Shenzhen, Guangdong Province, China
Completed: February 2010
P1_0210

Publisher's Cataloging-In-Publication Data
(Prepared by The Donohue Group, Inc.)

Patterson, Don, 1961-
    Dawson's down! / by Don Patterson ; illustrated by Sonny Schug.

    p. : col. ill. ; cm. -- (Tales of the RAF ; bk. 4)

    Originally published in 2000 by Hindsight Ltd.
    Summary: A bad dream causes twelve year old Harry Winslow to spend the night tossing and turning in his bed. Unfortunately, the next day becomes the real nightmare. Harry's friend, Erin, learns her father is missing in action. At the same time, Squadron Leader Captain Dawson is forced to bail out over the English Channel.
    Includes index.
    Interest age level: 007-010.
    ISBN: 978-1-936086-56-6 (hardcover/library binding)
    ISBN: 978-1-936086-62-7 (pbk.)

1. Great Britain. Royal Air Force--Juvenile fiction. 2. Fighter pilots--Great Britain--Juvenile fictio
3. World War, 1939-1945--Children--Great Britain--Juvenile fiction. 4. Spitfire (Fighter planes)--
Juvenile fiction. 5. Great Britain. Royal Air Force--Fiction. 6. Fighter pilots--Great Britain--Fict·
7. World War, 1939-1945--Children--Great Britain--Fiction. 8. Spitfire (Fighter planes)--Fiction. I
Schug, Sonny. II. Title. III. Series: Patterson, Don, 1961- Tales of the RAF ; bk. 4.

PZ7.P3884 Daw 2010
[Fic]   2009942883

To my wife, Joan.
She reminds us it's nice
to be important, but it's
more important to be nice.

TABLE OF CONTENTS

"DAWSON'S DOWN!"

CHAPTER ONE

A BAD DREAM

Filtering through the darkness, pale moonlight cast down on the silent farms and fields of Hampton County. While most of the English countryside slept through the quiet spring night, twelve year old Harry Winslow stirred in his bed. Awakened by a frightening nightmare, Harry tossed and turned, unable to fall back to sleep. Impatiently, the young boy waited for morning to come.

Finally, Harry noticed his room begin to brighten. Outside he heard roosters crow and a growing chorus of chirping songbirds. When sunlight spilled through his window, Harry breathed a sigh of relief. Night was over and a new day had arrived.

Short of sleep, Harry slowly climbed out from under his warm blankets and sat up on the edge of his bed. He rubbed his tired eyes and thought about his nightmare. Even though the ominous dream had been vivid enough to keep him up most the night, Harry could hardly make sense of it. Yet, convinced the nightmare was warning him about something, he tried his best to remember every detail.

But, Harry's thoughts shifted to breakfast when his house filled with the inviting smell of baked bread. Hungry from a restless night, he quickly reached for his clothes to get dressed. Still buttoning his shirt, Harry stumbled down the stairs and stepped into the kitchen.

Standing at the stove, Harry's mother was busy frying eggs. On the countertop next to her lay a plate stacked with steaming sausages and browned toast. Harry's empty stomach rumbled. Thankfully the kitchen table was already set, waiting for him.

"Good morning, little mister," Mrs. Winslow greeted Harry in a cheerful voice.

"Morning, Mom," Harry yawned while sitting down at the table.

Harry's mother couldn't help notice her son's drowsy tone and asked, "Did you sleep well, love?"

"No, I didn't," Harry complained. "I had the

oddest nightmare about Captain Dawson. In my dream he was a lamb lost in the field. Then a wolf pounced and grabbed him by the throat. I wanted to help, but I didn't know what to do. Luckily, the wolf let him go, but it frightened me so much, I woke up. After that, I couldn't get back to sleep." Harry scratched his head and mumbled, "I wish Dad was home, he could tell me what it all means."

Finished at the stove, Mrs. Winslow filled a plate with eggs and sausages and set it in front of Harry. Trying to console her son, she replied, "It was just a bad dream, sweetheart. I think maybe you've been spending too much time with Captain Dawson and the rest of your pilots on the airfield."

Hampton Airfield bordered the Winslow farm. Fascinated by the Royal Air Force squadron stationed there, Harry was a frequent visitor to the base. The Squadron Leader, Captain Dawson, and the rest 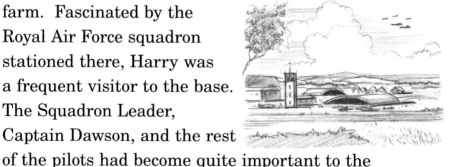 of the pilots had become quite important to the young boy.

Harry bit into his food and thought about his mother's remark. He knew she didn't always approve of the time he spent around the airfield. But what did a nightmare about lambs and wolves have to do with pilots and fighter planes? In Harry's mind, Hampton Airfield wasn't about nightmares, it stood for things like friendship, courage and honor.

Trying to avoid an argument, Harry quickly changed the subject. "Where's Sis?" he asked.

"Susan left for the airfield already," Mrs. Winslow sighed. "She's been spending a lot of time there lately. Either Colonel Harrison is working her too hard, or she's found something quite interesting."

Harry's older sister, Susan, worked at Hampton Airfield as Colonel Harrison's secretary. She enjoyed helping the Colonel administer the daily operation of the airbase, but it also gave her an opportunity to keep an eye on Harry.

At the mention of Hampton Airfield, Harry noticed the morning sunshine pouring through the kitchen window. The day was bright and clear. With good weather he knew the pilots would soon be scrambling to their fighter planes, ready to defend England.

Eager to join his RAF friends at the airfield,

Harry hurried with his breakfast. A familiar sight, Mrs. Winslow shook her head while watching her son race through his food.

Hoping to slow him down, his mother divulged, "Harry, love, I have a surprise. I've been waiting for the right time to give it to you. Maybe it will help you forget about that nightmare you had."

Excited, Harry quickly swallowed and asked, "What is it, Mom?"

Mrs. Winslow stepped to the cupboard, pulled out a box, and handed it to Harry. Harry ripped open the lid. When he looked inside, his eyes grew wide as saucers. Reaching in, he slowly pulled a white silk aviator's scarf from the box. Mrs. Winslow had sewn it by hand, and her work was exceptional.

"Mother, this is fantastic! No, it's magnificent! Thank you!" Harry shouted while wrapping the soft scarf around his neck.

Mrs. Winslow smiled at the heartfelt compliment from her son. "I'm glad you like it, dear. I made one for your pilot friend, Captain Dawson, too. After all, he's practically family. I hope it helps keep him warm when he is flying. You will give it to him for me, won't you?"

"Of course I will," Harry assured her. "He'll love his as much as I love mine."

Harry enjoyed the extra attention from his mother. The present she made was wonderful and indeed helped him forget his bad dream. Even better, thanks to her, he had something special to give Captain Dawson.

Harry gulped the very last of his breakfast and asked, "When I finish my chores can..."

"Yes, love, you can," Mrs. Winslow interrupted. "When you finish your chores you can go see your pilots."

CHAPTER TWO

A FRIEND IN NEED

Outside in the bright sunshine, Harry rushed to make quick work of his morning chores. Although most of his tasks around the farm were routine, he considered it his duty to make sure everything was done right. Harry's mother depended on him, and he knew it was important to do his best.

Caring for the small animals was Harry's favorite job. Every morning he fed the goats and lambs, and filled their trough with fresh drinking water. Then he took them out to pasture. The rest of the day, the ever-hungry animals followed Harry wherever they could, hoping for an extra handout.

Harry felt proud to be the seventh generation of Winslows to live in the small brick house and tend the land that was the Winslow farm. When he was younger, his father loved to tell him stories about their ancestors. His father, and his father's father as well as all the other generations had made their way in the world by raising sheep and tilling the very same soil.

Over the years, things had remained much the same for the people living in the countryside of Hampton County. That is, until war flared. Since late 1939, Harry's quiet life and everyone else's had changed. During that autumn, Harry's father left for London to help in the British government's Intelligence Service. And, the lush meadow where Harry and his father used to graze spring lambs was made into a landing strip for Royal Air Force fighter planes.

Out of place against the background of farm fields, the cluster of hangers and buildings of Hampton Airfield became a fixture in the landscape. Although the hazards of having an airbase nearby could be disquieting to the villagers, it was a time of war, and sacrifices were made by all. The RAF pilots risked their lives to protect their country. In return, the people of Hampton County defied the danger and tried to help the brave airmen anyway they could.

To young Harry Winslow, the pilots of Hampton's 14th Squadron were special. The men welcomed him into their tight knit fraternity of fighter pilots, and over time, Harry had proven himself worthy of their friendship. With his father away, they helped fill an emptiness in his heart.

Harry rushed through all his morning chores. Finished, he brushed the dust from his worn blue jacket, and straightened the ends of his new silk aviator's scarf. Carefully folding the scarf for Captain Dawson into a neat square, Harry started down the path leading to the airbase, excited to deliver the gift.

When Harry neared the bushy hedgerow fence that separated the Winslow farm from Hampton Airfield, he noticed someone sitting at the top of a small hill. The grassy knoll was Harry's favorite spot. Overlooking the hangers and airplanes parked out on the hardstand, it was a 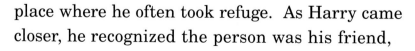 place where he often took refuge. As Harry came closer, he recognized the person was his friend,

Erin Bentley.

Ten year old Erin and her brother, Stuart, were Harry's best friends. Harry and Stuart were the same age and constant companions. But, Erin was the one who shared Harry's passion for the RAF pilots and planes. Settled in the long grass, Erin stared at the airfield.

"Hello, Erin," Harry called, and ran up the hill to join her.

Erin timidly waved, and replied softly, "Hello."

Harry sat down beside her. Almost instantly he could tell something was bothering Erin.

Worried about his friend, Harry tried to make conversation.

"Where's Stuart?" Harry asked, pretending to be cheerful.

"He's off visiting our grandparents in Manchester for the week," Erin explained. "Stuart gets a chance to be with Gram and Grampa for a while, and I get a few days alone with mother."

"That's great for both of you," Harry proclaimed. "A holiday, of sorts."

Erin just nodded her head and kept staring at the airfield.

After a long moment, she continued, "Mother and I had such a grand time planned. But, this morning she received word that father has been missing in action for three days. I've never seen her this worried before."

Mr. Bentley was a sergeant in the British Army stationed in North Africa. He had left his quiet life in Hampton County about the same time as Harry's father.

Although Harry knew first hand about the battle to defend his own country, all he knew about the war in the rest of the world was what he read in newspapers or heard on the radio.

Suddenly, now that his closest friend's father was missing on a continent far away, the reality of how the war affected everyone, everywhere, set in. It made Harry think of his own father and how much he missed him.

Harry nervously grabbed at the ends of his new silk scarf while searching for the right thing to say. Collecting his thoughts, he tried his best to console Erin.

"I'm sure your father is fine. He probably just got separated from his unit. Things will work out. They'll find him soon."

Erin shyly stared at the ground and smiled at Harry's reassuring words. Still, Erin was as concerned as her mother. Anxiously brushing the

 hair from her face, she looked at Harry. Then she noticed the silk scarf wrapped around his neck.

"Oh Harry, that's beautiful," she remarked. "Where did you get it?"

Harry smiled proudly. "It's an aviator's scarf. My mother made it for me. And, she made one for Captain Dawson. I was on my way to the airfield to give it to him."

Erin reached to feel the fabric. Running it through her fingers she giggled, "It's wonderful. Where did your mother get the silk to make it?"

Harry was stumped, he didn't know. Unable to answer, he just shook his head. All the while Erin continued to feel the material. Realizing how much she admired the scarf, Harry pulled it from his neck and handed her the length of white silk.

"Here," Harry offered, "try it on."

Erin wrapped the scarf around her neck. She rubbed the smooth, soft silk on her cheeks and held it up to the sun. Harry was glad to see the silken scarf bring a little cheer to his friend in her time of need.

"Keep it," Harry said.

Erin stopped and looked at Harry. "I can't keep this. It's too nice. Besides, your mother made it for you."

Holding the other scarf for Captain Dawson in his hand, Harry considered the situation. Thinking aloud, he explained, "My mother made these to help. That's what they're for. I think she would be happy to know you have it."

Before Erin could say anything else, her mother's voice echoed over the fields. Quickly throwing her arms around Harry, she hugged him tight. Then, Erin jumped up and ran off, calling, "My mom needs me, Harry. I'll see you later."

Harry watched Erin run to her mother. Erin and her brother, Stuart, were his closest friends. The three children relied on each other, especially in the worst of times. For years they had shared everything. This time, he shared her concern. Harry wished there was something he could do to help.

As Erin and her mother headed home, Harry continued on his way to the airfield. Slipping through the small gap in the hedgerow, he ran out to the hardstand looking for Captain Dawson. Harry could hardly wait to deliver his mother's present.

CHAPTER THREE

THE START OF A BAD DAY

Bright morning sunshine squeezed through the shuttered windows in the officer's quarters. Annoyed by the light, Captain Dawson rolled over in his bed and buried his head under the pillow. Still tired after a restless night, he had just fallen asleep when a loud knock rattled the door.

"Good morning Captains!" the base clerk called from outside. "Mission briefing in half an hour, at o'seven hundred."

Awakened by the pounding, Dawson's room-mate, Captain Simms, jerked his legs out from under the sheets and sat up on the side of his bed. Rested and ready to start the day, Simms shouted back to the clerk, "Thank you, Corporal, I got it. Mission briefing at o'seven hundred!"

Standing up from his bed, Captain Simms clenched his fists and stretched his arms wide. On the other side of the room he noticed Captain Dawson, still lying in his bunk.

"Come on Ted," Simms called. "Let's get

some breakfast before the briefing."

Dawson tossed in his bunk, and snapped back from under his pillow, "Go away. Let me sleep for ten more minutes."

"It's time to get cracking!" Simms urged his friend. "Besides, the skies are clear out there. We might have to scramble our planes in ten minutes. I want to get breakfast before it's too late."

Simms punctuated his message by throwing a pillow at Dawson and rocking his bunk.

"Okay Andy, you win," Captain Dawson complied in a weary voice. "There's no need to get nasty."

Rolling over in his bed, Dawson tossed the

pillow back to Simms. Slowly, the tired squadron leader slipped out from under his blankets and reached for his flight suit.

"I had the oddest dream last night," Dawson complained. "I couldn't get any sleep at all."

"What happened in this strange dream of yours?" Simms asked.

Dawson rubbed his eyes and started to tell the story. "I'm a goat..., no wait, actually I'm a lamb. Anyway, I get separated from the rest of the flock. Then a wolf grabs me in his clutches. Right when I think I'm sunk, the wolf lets me go." Dawson started scratching his head, and then muttered, "On top of that, I think Harry Winslow was there, too."

Simms thumbed his chin and stared at Dawson for a moment. "The Winslow boy was in your nightmare?" Simms brayed. "I think maybe you've been spending too much time with the lad."

"Bah," Dawson scoffed, "it was just a ropey dream."

Putting his hands on his hips, Simms declared, "A hot breakfast is what you need. It will do wonders for your disposition."

Dawson nodded his agreement and finished

getting dressed. Ready for breakfast, the RAF captains stepped out of their quarters and into the bright morning sunshine. Instinctively, they paused and looked up. After surveying the rich blue sky overhead, Dawson and Simms eyed each other. The two veteran fighter pilots knew it wouldn't be long before they would be flying.

CHAPTER FOUR

DANGEROUS ON THE GROUND

Hungry for breakfast, Dawson and Simms hurried to the mess hall. Inside, the rest of the pilots were already gathered around a table. The two captains quickly filled their plates with eggs and fried potatoes, then joined the others.

Settling into his chair, Captain Dawson watched the pilots feverishly racing through their morning meal. The men were so preoccupied with their food, they barely noticed their Squadron Leader and Captain Simms had joined them.

Dawson looked at Simms, embarrassed by the behavior of his fighter pilots. Then he realized it wasn't a lack of table manners, but the constant interruption of the "scramble" alarm that allowed little time for courtesy. The pilots had grown accustomed to being called to their planes as many as three and four times a day. A quick spoon and huge bites were essential to an RAF pilot hoping to complete a meal. Even conversation waited until after the entire group of men finished scooping the last morsels of food from their plates.

But once they had their fill, the pilots immediately started rattling off stories over cups of coffee and morning tea. Dawson and Simms sat quietly, listening to the men spin their yarns. Occasionally the two Captains would roll their eyes at each other, reacting to some of the more colorful and exaggerated tales that tumbled from the mouths of the younger pilots.

Soon the entire group focused on a light-hearted argument between Lieutenant James Hyatt and the ever mischievous Brian Gainey. Both pilots had recently received official credit for a "shared victory" over an enemy Heinkel bomber. And yet, Lieutenant Gainey's recollection of the battle completely dismissed any involvement on Hyatt's part. Not surprisingly, Lieutenant Hyatt's version of the story entirely excluded Gainey.

Almost instantly, the other pilots joined in the playful teasing. Captain Simms looked at Captain Dawson and gently shook his head. Dawson sat back in his chair. Holding a cup of tea to his lips, he tried to hide his laughter.

Lieutenant Gainey boldly detailed his story for the other pilots, "I was trailing behind the Heinkel's left wing and hit the engine with a short burst. Then I could see the tail gunner had me in his sights, so I rolled a bit right and lined up behind the other. I fired another quick squirt, and the second engine was in flames."

"That's rubbish!" Hyatt snapped. "The second engine was in flames because my bullets ripped it to shreds! I dropped practically 3,000 feet and came in on the right side of the bomber. A touch of the trigger, and I took out the engine and the rest of the wing with it."

"I don't think so, James," Gainey tauntingly disagreed. "It was just good flying on my part. I'll teach you how sometime."

Groans of disbelief went up from everyone around the table. The two young pilots continued arguing over the truth of their stories. Remaining silent, Simms and Dawson were satisfied to let the men have their fun.

"Brian, your story is just idiotic!" Lieutenant Hyatt shouted in an exasperated voice. "You were a mile away from that bomber when I flamed it!"

Throwing his arms wide to show Gainey's

The back of Hyatt's hand knocked Captain Dawson on the arm.

distance from the fight, the back of Hyatt's hand knocked Captain Dawson on the arm. Instantly, the boisterous crowd of pilots fell silent. When Hyatt turned to apologize for accidentally bumping Dawson, his jaw dropped. The cup Dawson was holding had spilled all over his suit.

Bathed in hot tea, Captain Dawson shouted, "Blast it all!"

"Oh, Captain... I... I am so sorry," Hyatt stammered. "Let me help you clean up."

Regaining his composure, Dawson replied, "It's all right, Lieutenant." Wiping at the spill with a napkin, he added, "My flight suit is already a little rank from the last few days of action anyway."

Seeing the look of panic in the young pilot's eyes, Dawson tried to relieve the tension by teasing, "Apparently you two are as dangerous on the ground as in the air. Just remember lads, I'm on your side!"

A burst of laughter from everyone at the table filled the room. Hardly missing a beat, the men quickly went back to their boastful stories. However, when Captain Simms looked at his watch and informed the group it was time for the morning briefing, the fleeting moment of fun ended. In practiced unison, the squadron of pilots stood up from their chairs. Still chatting, they started on their way to the Operations Building.

CHAPTER FIVE

ALL LEAVES ARE CANCELED

Captain Dawson and the rest of the squadron gathered together in the briefing room. While they waited for the base commander, the once playful pilots grew serious. Each day during the morning briefing, Colonel Harrison explained the objectives of Fighter Command, and assigned the squadron their mission duties. After that, the life of the RAF pilots was a daily gamble of life and death.

At precisely seven o'clock, Colonel Harrison entered the room. After a simple greeting, he promptly started the morning briefing.

"This is the latest report, gentlemen," Harrison explained while slowly pacing in front of the men. "The Germans have been pounding our ships in the channel, hard. As long as the weather holds, Fighter Command assumes they'll keep at us, tooth and nail. Unless we stop them, our supply lines will run dry and they'll have us by the throat. We've been ordered to maintain a full alert status, ready to scramble from dawn to dusk. In addition, the lads in the 27th and 79th Squadrons have had a pretty bad time of it, so we'll be covering some of their intercepts as well."

Harrison looked at the pilots for a moment and then announced, "Gentlemen, I'm sorry to say that with such a full plate, all leaves are canceled until further notice. No one is getting a holiday for a while. That is all. The scramble alarm will tell you when the time comes."

Their briefing finished, the squadron rose to attention and saluted Colonel Harrison. As the pilots left the room, the Colonel waved at Captain Dawson to get his attention.

"Ted...," Colonel Harrison started, but was then distracted by the dark stain covering Dawson's flight suit. "What happened to you, lad?"

Embarrassed by his appearance, Dawson sheepishly replied, "Just a bit of bad luck in the officer's mess."

Harrison eyed Dawson and commented wryly, "Well, it seems fitting. You are an officer, and you are a mess."

Dawson grew red faced.

"Now," Harrison continued, "what I wanted to know was, how many men are losing their weekend passes?"

"Well, Colonel...," Dawson replied, trying to hide his disappointment. "It seems I'm the only one. I had a four day leave coming up."

"Your day truly has started off a bit black, hasn't it?" Colonel Harrison said in an awkward tone. "But, cheer up, old man. I'll get you another leave as soon as things quiet down again. I know it's been quite a while since you've had a rest."

Dawson smiled and nodded his head. This wasn't the first time his leave had been canceled, and probably it wouldn't be the last. Even though the life of a fighter pilot was exhausting, Dawson knew his country depended on him, and men like him. Canceling a holiday was a small sacrifice. Dawson was prepared to fly and help defend England until the war was over.

CHAPTER SIX

THE SCRAMBLE ALARM

Finished with Colonel Harrison, Captain Dawson joined the rest of the pilots gathered out on the grassy airfield. Together, the unflappable group quietly waited for the sound of the scramble alarm.

The morning wore on while shadows of clouds silently slipped across the field. Passing the time, Captain Dawson watched the air crews and mechanics scurry about checking the readiness of the squadron of Hurricane and Spitfire fighter planes parked on the hardstand.

Glancing over at his own rugged Hurricane, Dawson noticed his trusty crew chief, Sergeant Pendleton, pacing back and forth between the tail and the engine of the airplane. Then Pendleton stopped and checked the landing gear. After that, he climbed onto the wing. Lifting the ammunition covers, he started examining the machine guns. When he finished fussing over the guns, Pendleton pulled out a handkerchief and began to polish the glass canopy.

Dawson was puzzled by Sergeant Pendleton's nervous preparation of the Hurricane. Even Captain Simms noticed the unusual display.

Leaning over to Dawson, Simms quietly asked, "What's up with Pendleton today?"

"I haven't a clue," Dawson whispered, "but I'd better go check."

By now, Sergeant Pendleton had started fiddling with the Hurricane's propeller. Calmly pretending nothing was wrong, Captain Dawson walked up and stood behind the stocky Sergeant. Unaware, Pendleton stepped back from the plane and bumped into Dawson.

"Excuse me, Captain," Pendleton apologized.

"That's quite all right, Sergeant," Dawson replied.

Together the two men stood quietly, looking at the sturdy fighter plane in front of them. Finally, Dawson broke the silence.

"Thomas, why are you fussing over my Hurricane this morning?"

"Just making sure everything is tip top, Captain!" Sergeant Pendleton replied.

Captain Dawson bent over to examine the

engine and grabbed at the fuel line. Pulling his
head away from the plane, Dawson looked directly
at Pendleton and asked, "Everything looks fine to
me. What has you so worried today?"

Kicking at the ground, Pendleton explained,
"I don't know. I just want to make sure everything
is perfect, so there's no problem when you're in
the thick of it."

Dawson put his arm on the mechanic's
shoulder. "I appreciate your effort, Thomas, but
it's just another day, like all the others. You've
kept me flying this long, there's no reason to think

30

today is any different."

"Yes, sir. If you say so, sir," Pendleton said in a disbelievingly tone. "But I have a feeling something bad could..."

Before another word passed between them, an alarm screamed across the airfield. The waiting was over. It was time to scramble the squadron. While the pilots raced to their fighter planes, aircrews started the thundering engines.

Climbing into the cockpit of his Hurricane, Captain Dawson had little time for Sergeant Pendleton's premonition. After a quick check of the plane's control surfaces, Dawson throttled up his engine. Looking down the row of Hurricanes and the three new Spitfires flown by Simms, Gainey and Hyatt, Dawson watched the smoky exhaust streaming from the popping engines. Impatiently, he waited for the last plane to turn over.

Then, Captain Dawson saw young Harry Winslow racing across the field. Harry ran up to the side of Dawson's Hurricane and in a winded voice shouted to the Captain.

"Captain Dawson!" Harry yelled over the roar of the churning propeller. "Please take this.

31

My mother made it for you."

Harry stretched to hand the silk aviator's scarf to Captain Dawson. The Squadron Leader grabbed the elegant white fabric and smiled. Quickly wrapping it around his neck and tucking the length into his flight suit, Dawson called to Harry.

"Harry, this is beautiful! Where did your mother find the fabric? Ever since the war, the only thing made of silk anymore is parachutes."

Harry shook his head and shouted back, "I don't know where she got the material. But she hopes it will help keep you warm when you're at high altitude."

Nodding his head Dawson exclaimed, "You know, Harry, your mother must have sacrificed a lot to make this. Tell her thank you for me."

Ready to go, Captain Dawson signaled for Sergeant Pendleton to pull the chocks from his wheels. "Stand back now, Harry. We've got a job to do. I'll see you in an hour or so."

Surrounded by the roar of aircraft engines and preoccupied with leading the mission, Dawson couldn't hear Harry when the boy shouted back, "I wish I could help, too."

The Captain closed his canopy, and waved goodbye one last time. Adjusting his headgear, Dawson could feel the soft silk scarf cushion his chin. Outside, Harry stepped back from the airplane and turned away from the swirling dust kicked up by the churning propeller.

Strapped in his cockpit, Captain Dawson keyed the radio, "Squadron ready?"

Dawson's voice sounded more like a command than a question. A moment later, the eleven other pilots all checked in. Keying his radio one more time Dawson announced, "Gentlemen, we're off!"

In response, the pilots throttled up their engines and started to pull away from the hardstand. The deafening roar from the squadron of RAF fighter planes echoed across the countryside. Racing down the airfield in flights of three, the mix of nine rugged Hurricanes and three new

Spitfires hurled over the turf and climbed into the blue sky.

Back at the Winslow house, the thunder of airplane engines rattled the windows. Inside, Mrs. Winslow stopped her sewing long enough to think of Captain Dawson and the rest of his pilots. Quietly she wished for their safety, and returned to her stitching.

CHAPTER SEVEN

INTERCEPT

Captain Dawson radioed Fighter Command and asked for the location of the incoming enemy aircraft. According to the flight controller at Section Headquarters, the RAF radar network had picked up a large German formation when it cleared the French coastline headed for England.

"Roger, Command," Dawson replied, "German formation at twenty-five miles out, heading due west."

Adjusting course, Captain Dawson led his squadron to intercept the German planes before they could attack any English ships sailing through the English Channel. Racing at top speed, the group of Hurricanes and Spitfires would engage the enemy in less than five minutes.

"Keep your eyes open, lads," Dawson called to the others while searching the sky around him. "Intercept in two minutes."

Below the RAF fighter formation, a convoy of ships traced curved white lines on the blue water of the English Channel. Counting the number of freighters steaming to harbor, Dawson mumbled to himself, "There's plenty of shipping down there for them to be going after."

Anticipating the incoming German planes, tense seconds slowly ticked away. But, when Dawson's headset sparked with a message from one of his pilots, the anxious moments ended.

"Bandits, 12 o'clock low!"

Dawson jerked in his seat and squinted through his canopy. Below him and to the right, a group of German aircraft dotted the sky. Straining to identify the type and number of enemy planes, he counted twelve large aircraft surrounded by eight smaller ones.

Dawson called to the other members of his squadron, "I count twelve bombers and eight fighter escort. Can anyone confirm that?"

"That's right, Captain," Lieutenant Gainey replied. "I confirm twelve Stukas and eight Messerschmitts flying escort, straight ahead."

Dawson adjusted his goggles and flipped

the safety latch off the gun trigger on his control stick. Briefly looking right, he could see Simms and some of the other pilots preparing for combat in the same manner.

"Get ready to mix it up, gentlemen," Dawson declared. "Break on my mark!" Eager to protect the convoy of English ships below, Captain Dawson shouted into his radio, "Break!"

Throwing the yoke hard right, Dawson rolled his Hurricane on its side and dropped toward the Luftwaffe formation. Simms, Gainey and Hyatt, flying the new Spitfires, followed their Squadron Leader on a long diving approach to attack the enemy bombers. But, the vicious German fighter escort swarmed on the remaining Hurricanes.

Gaining speed as they hurled earthward, the distance between the four British fighters and the German Stukas rapidly closed. Dawson trained his guns on the enemy dive bombers, but the Stuka in front of him suddenly dropped away, out of his gunsight. Amazed at how quickly the bomber disappeared, he realized the Stukas were diving to attack the ships below.

"The Stukas are diving!" Dawson yelled into the radio. "Hurry up lads. The Stukas are diving!"

Dawson...pitched forward in an even steeper dive.

The flight of German dive bombers all nosed down in unison, dropping in a straight line for the unsuspecting English freighters steaming through the choppy water below. Dawson struggled to correct his course in order to pursue the diving German planes.

In a bold attempt to reach the bombers before they could attack the ships, Dawson twisted his Hurricane and pitched forward in an even steeper dive. The force of the plunge pushed Dawson back in his seat. On the gauges in front of him, the air speed indicator passed 400 miles per hour, into the red zone of the dial. The turbulent rush of air passing over the control surfaces on the wings of his Hurricane rattled the stick in his hands.

Behind Dawson, Simms and the other two Spitfires endured much the same as they followed in pursuit of the German bombers. Without hesitation, the Spitfire pilots committed themselves to the perilous dive in order to save the British ships from the attacking Germans. All the while above them, the rest of the pilots of the 14th Squadron continued to battle the ferocious squad of German Me 109 fighters.

Dawson glanced up into the mirror on his canopy. Reflected in the glass, the three Spitfires

matched his every move as he raced to intercept the deadly German Stukas. Hurling toward the bombers, as well as the ocean surface, Dawson and the others could afford little time to strike and then pull out of their dizzying dive.

Concentrating on the line of enemy planes, Dawson ignored the ocean waves in front of him. Struggling with his controls, he aligned his gunsight on the lead bomber. Time was running out. Any mistake at this point and he would crash into the icy water below.

"It's now or never," Dawson mumbled to himself and triggered his guns at the first Stuka. At the same moment, Simms, Gainey and Hyatt fired into the line of enemy planes. Tracers from the guns of all four RAF fighters flew into the formation of dive bombers. With them, a rain of bullets smashed into the diving German planes.

Captain Dawson jerked back on the control

stick with every ounce of strength he could muster.
Sweat beaded on his brow and seeped into his eyes.
Blinded by the stinging perspiration, he couldn't
see the ocean surface edging dangerously closer.
Straining every muscle while pulling back on the
yoke, his Hurricane finally leveled out of its long
dive and began to climb back into the sky.

Regaining his senses, Dawson twisted in his
seat to survey the situation around him. Scattered
about, the broken formation of Luftwaffe planes
desperately tried to gain altitude. Smoke trailed
behind two of the Stukas still flying. Below, the
smashed hulk of one German bomber bobbed on
the surface of the water. Two others had already
passed below the frothing ocean waves.

White against the rich blue sky, a group of
parachutes caught Dawson's attention. After
jumping from their crippled planes, the German
airmen drifted toward the
water. Below them, the
convoy of British cargo
ships continued on their
way to port, unharmed.

CHAPTER EIGHT

"DAWSON'S DOWN!"

Captain Dawson circled the area above the group of freighters making their way through the water. Soon, the three Spitfires piloted by Captain Simms and Lieutenants Gainey and Hyatt had joined him. Together, the four RAF fighters watched over the ships steaming to safe harbor on the English coast.

Simms radioed to Dawson, "You don't plan to lead us on another dive like that again in the near future, do you?"

Dawson wiped the sweat from his forehead and replied, "No, Andy. At least I hope not. For a moment there, I was regretting the fact I never learned how to swim."

Catching his breath, Dawson continued, "Okay, gentlemen, the holiday is over. We better get back up and help the lads with those Me 109s."

Above, the rest of the squadron continued their dogfight with the German Messerschmitts. At full throttle, the four RAF planes raced to join the others. But the Spitfires, with their more powerful engines and advanced design, were climbing faster than Dawson's rugged Hurricane. Realizing his friend was lagging behind, Captain Simms purposely held back to provide support for the slower plane.

Trailing after Hyatt and Gainey, Dawson and Simms were the last to approach the battling fighter planes. Focused on the heated skirmish above, Dawson was surprised when a flash of bullets hurled past his cockpit. Frantically searching for the source of the gunfire, the RAF captain realized a German Me 109 had lined up behind him.

Caught while struggling to gain altitude, Dawson was an easy target. And yet, the German fighter all but ignored the vulnerable Hurricane. Seeking the prize of downing a Spitfire, the greedy Messerschmitt pilot fixed his sights on Simms and opened fire. Trying to escape, Simms poured on the throttle to his engine. But the sleek enemy plane continued to bare down on the Spitfire, tracing its every move.

Amazed how the German pilot continued to ignore his Hurricane, Dawson was determined to

put such error in judgment to good use. Throwing his controls from side to side, the Squadron Leader tried to reposition himself on the Me 109 stalking the twisting Spitfire.

"Andy," Dawson radioed, "jink away and I'll follow behind!"

"Roger," Simms replied.

Simms rolled his Spitfire along a dizzying path, successfully dodging a rain of bullets from the Me 109 long enough for Dawson to take aim. When the Messerschmitt lined up in his crosshairs, Captain Dawson fired. Bullets from the Hurricane's guns pounded on the Me 109's engine housing. Smoke began to spew from the exhaust ports. Losing power, the crippled German fighter fell away from the RAF planes.

However, no sooner had Dawson saved Simms, than his own life was in peril. The time spent pursuing the Me 109 threatening Simms left Dawson open to attack. Taking advantage of the situation, another Messerschmitt now hunted the Hurricane. Unfortunately for Dawson, this

German pilot had no intention of letting him out of his sights.

Suddenly, bullets from the Me 109 smashed through Dawson's canopy and into the front of his plane. The pistons in his engine started to grind until the rods snapped. Oil and smoke began pouring from the exhausts.

Captain Dawson and his Hurricane struggled for survival. A few more hits from the German Messerschmitt, and the beaten fighter would most likely burst into flames. In desperation, Dawson rolled over and started to dive trying to escape the final fury of the Me 109.

Smoke filled the cockpit, and wind whistled through the shattered glass canopy as the crippled Hurricane twisted earthward. Dawson shouted into his radio, hoping someone would hear.

"I'm bailing out! I'm bailing out!"

Instantly, Dawson's headset sparked with messages returning from the other pilots, "Roger, Dawson's down!"

Plummeting through the sky, Captain Dawson had no time to respond. The forceful spin of the airplane made every move that much harder to make. Each thought was that much more

...before his headset pulled from its plug, Dawson heard one last message...

confusing. Pulling at the lever, he struggled to open the canopy. Unstrapping the belts to his seat and crawling out of the cockpit, Dawson lifted his legs over the side and onto the bullet riddled wing of his Hurricane.

Just before his headset pulled from its plug, Dawson heard one last message that brought him some comfort. The voice of his closest friend, Captain Simms, crackled, "Ted, I'm coming. I'll follow you down."

Dawson grabbed the release ring to his parachute. Tearing the pin from his chest pack, he could feel the pull of the fabric as it spilled into the sky. Suddenly, the bundle of silk and cords filled with air, violently yanking him away from the twisting airplane.

Dawson watched his feet clear from the wing and then felt a sharp pain in his head. His vision narrowed to darkness. The last thing he recognized was the spiraling tail of his Hurricane falling toward the choppy waters of the English Channel. Unconscious, Dawson's limp body drifted through the bright blue sky, down to the cold waves below.

CHAPTER NINE

THE SQUADRON RETURNS

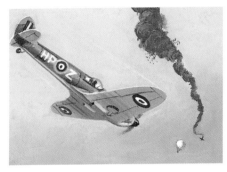

Unsuccessful at damaging any allied ships, the German raiders turned east and headed home. While the rest of the squadron patrolled the sky looking for any remaining enemy planes, Captain Simms followed the trail of smoke left by Dawson's battered Hurricane. Searching the area, Simms felt a wave of relief when he spotted the open parachute of his wounded friend. And yet, flying in his Spitfire, all he could do was helplessly watch the drifting pilot float down and settle into the sea.

Circling over the patch of ocean where Dawson hit the water, Simms realized he couldn't watch over the downed Squadron Leader for long. Low on fuel, he and the other RAF pilots would have to leave the area before they could ensure his safety. Simms urgently radioed Coastal

48

Command to inform them of Dawson's location. Hopefully, they would quickly launch a rescue and return him to Hampton before dark.

It was up to Captain Simms, as second in command, to lead the remaining planes in Dawson's absence. He was the Squadron Leader now. Weighing the safety of the rest of the men against that of one downed pilot, Simms knew he had to order the squadron to return to Hampton. The RAF pilots were a family. Abandoning a fellow flier was painful, but sometimes necessary. Short of fuel and ammunition, if enemy fighters were to attack now, the entire squadron would be lost.

After contacting Coastal Command, Simms ordered his pilots to return home. As the squadron turned west without Dawson, the heart of each pilot sank. Nothing more was said for the rest of the flight.

Less than twenty minutes later, the planes of the 14th Squadron roared over Hampton Airfield. On the ground, the command officers looked up to the sky and the aircrews rushed out

to the hardstand. While the Hurricanes and
Spitfires approached the field to land, Colonel
Harrison automatically counted the planes.
Alarmed to see only eleven returning, he headed
to the airfield looking for answers.

The pilots landed their thundering fighters
on the grassy runway and taxied to the hardstand.
With the usual flurry of activity upon their
return, flight crews swarmed on the planes.
Before the propellers stopped spinning, the eager
mechanics set to work refueling the tanks and
rearming the guns.

Spent from the mission, Captain Simms
slowly rolled back the canopy to his Spitfire and
jumped to the ground. The other pilots raced
across the hardstand to talk to him. Noticing the
frenzy, Colonel Harrison stopped short of the
field. From the distance, Harrison searched the
mob of pilots for Captain Dawson.

"Surely," Harrison said to himself, "Dawson
can explain what's going on."

On the hardstand, Captain Simms stood
among the rush of people wanting to know what
happened. Even the ground crews were asking
about Dawson. Simms grew hoarse trying to explain.

While answering all of the questions thrown at him, he noticed something that made him stop.

On the other side of the hedgerow fence stood Harry Winslow. Simms could see the young boy's eyes search the crowd gathered on the hard-stand. Without a doubt, he knew Harry was looking for Captain Dawson. Simms also knew Harry was searching in vain.

When Harry's eyes met Captain Simms', the fact that Dawson hadn't returned with the squadron became painfully apparent to both the boy and the veteran pilot. Standing alone on the

hill, Harry's knees went weak and tears swelled in his eyes. His most special friend, Captain Dawson, was lost. Sadness devoured the twelve year old. Desperate for comfort, Harry turned and raced home.

Simms watched the broken-hearted boy run back up the dirt path leading away from the airfield. Frustrated and angry, he turned from the mournful crowd and whipped his head gear to the ground. Tired of the chaos on the hardstand, Simms stormed off to meet Colonel Harrison and explain the situation.

CHAPTER TEN

THE SACRIFICE

Harry Winslow ran the entire way back to his house and bolted up the stairs. Winded from running so far, Harry struggled to catch his breath. Tears poured down his cheeks.

Hearing the clamor, Mrs. Winslow called for her son. "Harry, what's wrong? What happened?"

Harry timidly entered the room where his mother was sitting with her sewing. Standing in the doorway trying to be strong, Harry collected himself and started to explain. "The squadron is back. But, Captain Dawson wasn't...he didn't..."

Mrs. Winslow looked up from her needle and thread. Harry's tears and his brief explanation were enough to tell her what happened. Hoping to soothe her hurting son, she held her arms out inviting him to sit on her lap. Without hesitation, Harry ran to his mother. Mrs. Winslow held him tight. But even in her warm embrace, Harry couldn't stop crying.

"Sweetheart," Mrs. Winslow started in a

soft voice, "Captain Dawson has been fighting to save Britain for a long time. He's sacrificed much in order to help us all."

Harry nodded his head. Through his tears, he added, "Erin's father is missing, too."

"I know, Harry," Mrs. Winslow said softly. "I spoke with Erin's mother earlier. Thankfully, the Bentleys and Captain Dawson have faith and hope on their side. But we must help, too."

"What can we do?" Harry mourned.

Hesitating for a moment to think, she replied, "You see, Harry, what's important isn't always what we do to help, but that we are willing to do what we can. Even if that means we must sacrifice a bit of ourselves. Our hearts will tell us best what to do when the time comes."

Harry listened closely to his mother's brave words, but they did little to make him feel better. He couldn't believe both Erin's father and Captain Dawson were lost, and still worse, at the same time. While the clock on the wall ticked away, Harry and his mother sat quietly in the comfort of each other's arms.

Suddenly, the door to the house flew open. Harry's sister, Susan, had rushed home from

Colonel Harrison's office with important news.
Susan dashed from room to room looking for her
brother. Racing through the house she shouted,
"Harry, Captain Dawson is alive!"

Relieved, Mrs. Winslow quickly called, "Susan,
we're up here in the sewing room."

When Susan found Harry and her mother
she eagerly announced, "I overheard Captain
Simms reporting to Colonel Harrison. Captain
Dawson was shot down, but he bailed out of his
plane in time. He's alive somewhere in the water
off the coast."

Harry jumped from his mother's lap, shouting, "Sis, that's wonderful news!"

"It is certainly the most wonderful news,"
Mrs. Winslow agreed. "I'll go downstairs and put
on a pot of tea and you can tell us all about it."

After Mrs. Winslow left for the kitchen,
Harry looked at Susan and asked, "When will
Captain Dawson be picked up?"

Susan took a deep breath. The excitement
drained from her face.

"Harry," Susan explained, "Captain Dawson
is alive, but there's a problem. There's so much
German activity in the channel that Coastal
Command can't risk sending anyone to pick him
up right now."

"But, Susan," Harry shot back, "if they
don't rescue him soon, he could die out there."

Susan took Harry's hand, "Harry, right now
even more people could die trying to reach Captain
Dawson. That's the last thing he would want."

Harry looked at Susan. He understood the
problem, but wanted Captain Dawson safe, just
the same.

"Colonel Harrison will find a way to get
Captain Dawson back," she finished, trying to offer

some hope.

With that, Susan left to help Mrs. Winslow in the kitchen. Alone in his mother's sewing room, Harry sat down in her rocking chair to think. He desperately wanted to help, but didn't know how.

Looking around the room, Harry eyed some of his mother's sewing projects. A pile of socks to be darned and some shirts in need of new buttons were heaped on the floor. Then, some long strips of the same silk his mother used to make the aviator scarves caught his attention. Thumbing through the pieces, he counted eleven lengths. Harry's mother had cut enough fabric to make a scarf for each member of the squadron.

Still thinking about Dawson, Harry started to rub the smooth silk between his fingers. Looking up, he noticed his mother's old wedding gown laying on the table. Harry remembered how much she loved that dress. Every year on his parent's wedding anniversary she took it out of the box and showed it to his father. She would hold it in front of her and dance around the room. Just then, Harry realized he had forgotten something. Today was his parent's wedding anniversary!

Harry looked closer at the wedding dress. He could tell something was wrong. In the past, it had always been carefully laid out. This time it was spread apart and cut into pieces. When he saw that the the long silk train of the beautiful gown had been cut away, he realized where his mother had gotten the fabric for his scarf. Mrs. Winslow used her precious gown to help Harry and the pilots of the 14th Squadron in her own way.

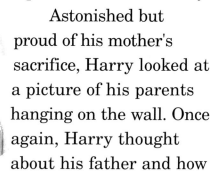

Astonished but proud of his mother's sacrifice, Harry looked at a picture of his parents hanging on the wall. Once again, Harry thought about his father and how much he missed him. He was confident his dad would know what to do in a time like this.

Staring at the family portrait, Harry suddenly had an idea. Realizing he found the answer, Harry bolted down the stairs and flew out the door shouting to his mother and sister, "I know who can help Captain Dawson!"

CHAPTER ELEVEN

THE LIFE RAFT

Barely able to open his eyes, a dazed Captain Dawson struggled to concentrate through the numbness in his head. Ever so slowly his senses started to return. Looking up, Dawson made out wispy clouds in the sky. He recognized the smell and bitter taste of salt water. When he noticed his head rocking back and forth, Dawson was startled to realize he was floating on a raft in the ocean.

"Hello my Cap-i-tan," a distinct voice called.

Confused by his whereabouts, Dawson focused on the sounds echoing in his head. Dizzy from a concussion suffered while jumping from his Hurricane, he lay still, listening to the voice calling him.

"Hello my Cap-i-tan."

This time, the words came clearer. Dawson's senses were finally reaching the point of being useful, even capable of telling him about his surroundings. But, a sinking feeling of fear caused his entire body to tense when he started to understand the situation. Captain Dawson was floating in a life raft somewhere in the English Channel, with someone.

"Hello my Cap-i-tan. I am glad to see you are still with me, yes?"

The thick German accent and broken English spoken by the other person in the raft sent chills up Dawson's spine. The man sitting across from him was German, most likely the pilot of an enemy plane he, or one of his men, shot down. Instinctively, the RAF Squadron Leader reached for his side arm. Dawson's sudden movement sent a wave of crippling pain through his body, ending with a sickening pounding in his head.

"I'm afraid you will find your gun is missing," the German pilot explained. "I tossed it into the water. I have found that guns and rubber life rafts do not mix, yes? It could make a hole."

Captain Dawson stopped searching for his weapon. Defiantly, he replied, "No matter. A British ship will soon be here to rescue me. I must advise you that you are now my prisoner."

The German pilot let out a hardy laugh. Leaning over to Dawson he spoke in a soft but firm tone, "I'm afraid, Captain, that you are my prisoner. Soon a German U-boat will pick us up, and you will be sent to one of our fine prisoner-of-war camps."

Sitting up in the raft, Dawson squinted in the bright sunlight while he studied the man across from him. The face of the German pilot had fine features topped by thick, lightly colored hair. The insignias on his tan flight suit indicated he was a Luftwaffe group leader of some sort. Dawson guessed at the man's age. Although he was probably in his mid twenties, the worn look on the German's face made him seem older than his years.

"You forget, old chap, this is the English Channel," Dawson reminded his raft mate.

The other pilot laughed once more. "We shall make a bet, you and me, about who rescues us first. We will consider it a friendly wager..., between enemies."

While the German spoke, a sparkle of light

reflected from the buckle of his belt. The darting flashes caught Dawson's attention, and the grim reality of the situation struck him full force. Strapped to the German pilot's belt was a holster. In the holster rested a pistol. For now, the German was right, Dawson was his prisoner.

Resigned to the situation, Dawson asked, "How did I get here?"

The Luftwaffe pilot put his hands on his knees in preparation to tell the story. Dawson noticed the man's hands were raw and swollen. Obviously in pain, the German remained calm and cool-headed. Even though the other pilot was considered the enemy, for some reason, Dawson was beginning to feel he wasn't a threat.

"You dropped into the water over there," the Luftwaffe pilot started to explain while pointing at the spot. "I could see your head bobbing in the waves. When your parachute fell into the sea, it started to drag you down. I paddled the raft over to you and unstrapped the parachute. Then, I grab your suit and pull you from the water. So we are here together now, yes?"

Dawson listened to the German's story. The last thing he remembered was jumping from his crippled Hurricane and hitting his head on the tail. As the memory slowly came back to him, Dawson lifted his hand to his aching head.

"When I bailed out, I hit my head on the tail of my plane," Dawson recalled. "Then I blacked out."

"Yes, your head. You have a very big bump," the enemy pilot replied.

After a long pause, the German wryly asked Dawson, "Are you not going to ask me how I got here?"

Captain Dawson looked into the soft blue eyes of the German officer. He already knew the answer, but preferred to avoid it. Dawson was confident the man was the pilot of a plane he shot down just before his own plane was hit. He worried that discussing the situation might agitate the otherwise friendly German. Dawson decided it best to say nothing but simply wait to be rescued by someone. Hopefully, someone English.

CHAPTER TWELVE

CALL FOR HELP

Harry raced back down the path, across the airfield and into the Operations Building. Without even a knock at the door to announce himself, the twelve year old burst into Colonel Harrison's office. Inside, Captain Simms stood over Harrison's desk while the Colonel was talking to someone on the telephone.

Startled by Harry's abruptness, Captain Simms turned and glared at the boy. Putting his finger to his lips, Simms signaled for Harry to be quiet. Meanwhile, Colonel Harrison argued with the person on the other end of the phone line.

"I want my pilot back!" Harrison barked into the receiver. "I want Captain Dawson picked up now!"

Colonel Harrison gripped the telephone tightly, expecting a response. Suddenly, he shouted, "Wait!"

Looking defeated, the Colonel sat down in his chair and mindlessly tapped the phone in his hand. Finally he hung it up and stared at Captain Simms.

"I'm sorry, Andy, Coastal Command is under orders. The Germans have at least thirty U-boats operating in the English Channel right now. It's too dangerous. They won't send anyone to pick up Dawson until the threat from those submarines is gone."

Simms turned around to face the Colonel, revealing Harry Winslow at his side.

"Harry," the Colonel snapped, "what are you doing here?"

Harry shrank back from the terse tone of Colonel Harrison. Noticing the fearful look on Harry's face, Harrison realized he was being too hard on the young boy. Knowing how close Harry was to Captain Dawson, he started to apologize.

"I'm sorry, lad. Keep in mind that Dawson's all right, just a little wet floating about the channel. But, I must admit, we're having a time of it trying to get him plucked from the water."

Harry straightened up and replied, "I understand, Colonel. The whole English Channel is swarming with German submarines right now. Susan told me."

Impatiently, Captain Simms suggested, "Try again, Colonel. Perhaps we could go to someone higher up at Fighter Command this time."

"Andy, I've already tried the Air Vice Marshall! I've also called Coastal Command Headquarters and even some of the local fishing boats. It's just too dangerous out there. I don't know of anyone else who can help us."

Harry stepped to the front of Colonel Harrison's desk. "Colonel, I know someone."

Captain Simms and Colonel Harrison looked

hard at young Harry. Then the two RAF veterans eyed each other, wondering who Harry could possibly know with enough influence to order the rescue of Captain Dawson from the English Channel.

Harrison crossed his arms over his broad chest and asked, "Who do you know that can help us, lad?"

Harry swallowed and nervously answered, "My father, Trevor Winslow. He works in the Intelligence Service. I'm sure he would try to help."

Colonel Harrison's jaw dropped. Astonished, Captain Simms just stood there looking at Harry. Harrison struggled to regain his composure.

"You mean to tell us that your father is Trevor Winslow? Sir Trevor Winslow of the British Intelligence Service?"

Harry felt a little uneasy at the way Colonel Harrison was asking about his father. "Well..., yes sir, that's my father."

Then Captain Simms knelt down and asked the boy, "Do you know what your father does in London?"

Harry shook his head and answered, "Not really, but I think he knows a lot of people in the government. Maybe they could help."

Simms turned and looked at Harrison. The two men were speechless.

"Harry," Colonel Harrison explained, "your father, Trevor Winslow, is one of the Prime Minister's chief advisors. If anything were to happen to Mr. Churchill, your father would most likely become the new leader of England."

Harry was amazed. He knew his father worked with the government, but had no idea how important he was.

"Then he really can help us," Harry replied. "We must call him right now."

Colonel Harrison picked up the phone and dialed the number for Trevor Winslow's office in London. A secretary answered.

"Would you please tell Mr. Winslow that Colonel Harrison is on the line?" Harrison asked.

The secretary curtly replied, "Colonel, Mr. Winslow is in a meeting. I will tell him you called."

Harrison frowned and barked into the phone, "But this is a matter of life and death."

"Colonel," the secretary argued, "there's a war going on. Every matter is one of life or death. I'm sure Mr. Winslow will get back to you within a couple days."

Before Colonel Harrison could respond, there was a click and the phone went silent. Mr. Winslow's secretary had hung up. Unsure of what to do, Harrison looked at Simms and Harry. Sheepishly, he tried to explain, "She said he'll call back and then hung up the line."

"Ring her up again," Captain Simms immediately suggested.

Harry nodded his head and added, "Colonel, this time tell her Sir Harry of Hampton is calling."

Doubtful a silly nickname would bear any weight, Harrison reluctantly dialed the number once more. When the secretary picked up the phone, he demanded to speak with Harry's father.

"This is Colonel Harrison again. I must speak to Mr. Winslow."

"I'm sorry, sir," the secretary apologized, "but Mr. Winslow is in a meeting with the Prime Minister, Mr. Churchill. I can't interrupt them."

Harrison quickly replied, "Would you please tell him Sir Harry of Hampton is on the line."

"Sir Harry of Hampton?" the secretary asked. "Of course, sir. Please wait one moment, Colonel."

Colonel Harrison was amazed at the abrupt change in the secretary's temperament. Before the Colonel could catch his breath, there came a voice from the other end of the telephone.

"Harry? Is it really you?"

Startled, Colonel Harrison quickly handed the phone to Harry.

"Father? Are you there? I need your help."

Excited to hear his father's voice, Harry clung to the receiver with both hands. Brought together by telephone, the two Winslows began to talk.

"Harry, how are you, and Susan, and your mother?" Mr. Winslow asked.

"We're fine," Harry replied. "But we need your help. Captain Dawson has been shot down over the Channel, but Coastal Command can't pick him up."

"There's a lot of enemy activity out there right now, Harry. I've been tracking it for days," Mr. Winslow explained. "The Germans have made it quite dangerous for everyone."

"But Dad," Harry pleaded, "Captain Dawson is out there."

A military intelligence officer, Mr. Winslow was well aware of Captain Dawson's reputation as an exceptional and valuable Royal Air Force pilot. He was also aware of Dawson's special friendship with Harry.

After a brief pause, Mr. Winslow replied, "I understand, Harry, I'll try my best."

Harry nodded his head, comforted by his father's help. Then he asked, "There's another thing. Erin's father has been missing in North Africa for three days. Can you find out what's happened to him?"

"Bentley is missing? I'll make some calls and try my best," Mr. Winslow replied.

"One other thing," Harry hesitantly added. "Can you come home? I..., I mean, we all miss you so much. Remember, it's your anniversary. Could you take a holiday and come home? It would mean so much to mother."

Mr. Winslow struggled

to explain. "Harry, I would like to come home, but Mr. Churchill and the rest of our lads need my help. Besides, I can't look into those other matters and come home at the same time. I'm sorry, but you'll have to tell me what is most important."

Harry thought for a brief moment. The vision of his mother's wedding dress, and the sacrifice she had made ran through his head. He worried about Captain Dawson drifting in the English Channel. Then he thought of Erin's father missing in the African desert. Harry desperately wanted to see his father, but he knew his friends needed Mr. Winslow's help even more. A sacrifice had to be made.

"Pick up Captain Dawson and find out about Erin's father," Harry said. "Those are the most important things to do."

"All right, Harry. I'll try my best," Mr. Winslow replied. "I have to go now. Tell your mother and sister I love them. And as for you, young man, you make me very proud. Always remember I love you, too."

Harry nodded his head and smiled at his father's words. Listening to the click of the phone hanging up on the other end, he suddenly felt lonely. Reluctantly, Harry handed Colonel Harrison the receiver. It was hard for him to let go of the line that had carried the voice of his father.

CHAPTER THIRTEEN

HELPING HANDS

Over eight hours had passed since Captain Dawson bailed out of his crippled Hurricane and was saved from drowning by the German pilot. Soaking wet, the strong breeze and cold water chilled Dawson to the bone. It was impossible for the men to stay dry while the churning waves of saltwater washed over the sides of the small rubber raft keeping the two enemy pilots afloat.

Still dazed from his head wound, Captain Dawson struggled to stay awake. Even though the German officer saved his life, Dawson felt it wise to remain wary. Trying to keep his wits about him, he searched for something to talk about. Then Dawson noticed the burned hands of the Luftwaffe pilot. By the way he was holding them, it was clear the man was in severe pain.

"Can I help you?" Dawson asked, looking at the swollen hands.

"The ocean salt has proven most painful," the German winced. "But I have no medical supplies. Not even a bandage to cover them."

Dawson thought for a moment. Quick with an idea, he grabbed the silk scarf from around his neck and pulled it from his flight suit. Careful to keep the fabric clear of the saltwater, he started to rip the special gift from Mrs. Winslow into long strips. After tearing the scarf in two, he reached into his pocket and pulled out a small canteen of fresh water.

Cautiously, Captain Dawson reached for the German's hands. The wounded pilot reluctantly allowed Dawson to hold his puffy fingers and blistered palms. In order to wash away the salt, Dawson slowly poured some water from his canteen over the burns. Biting pain caused the German to pull back. But, as the fresh water washed away the salt, the sting started to fade.

Dawson wrapped the lengths of silk torn from his scarf around the German's burned hands. Gently, the English pilot tied the ends of the strips to secure them. His pain slightly relieved, the German officer smiled at Dawson and relaxed against the side of the raft.

"Why do you choose to help me so?" the Luftwaffe pilot asked.

"The same reason you saved me from drowning," Dawson replied.

The German pilot looked at Dawson sternly, "I saved you because I am an officer in the Luftwaffe! I don't just watch people drown without helping."

Dawson shifted, trying to sit up, "I am an officer in the Royal Air Force. I don't sit and watch people suffer without helping."

The two men sat quietly, each considering what the other had said. Finally, the German broke the silence.

"Perhaps... Perhaps we are not that different after all."

Dawson nodded his head and politely introduced himself. "I am Captain Ted Dawson. Thank you for saving me from drowning."

The German pilot looked at Dawson. "I am Captain Gerhardt Mueller. Thank you for your help. My hands, they are no longer in such pain."

The men started to talk with each other, slowly at first. After a while, the two pilots were exchanging stories about growing up and learning how to fly. Alone in a raft, far away from home, it was easy for Dawson and Mueller to forget they were enemies.

Another hour passed, and the two downed pilots anxiously bided their time. Waiting to be rescued from the cold sea was hard enough. Worrying about who would retrieve the raft first made it even harder. As the sun slipped lower on the horizon, both men started running out of patience and hope.

Suddenly, the choppy water around the raft started to boil. From beneath the waves a large black object pushed its way to the surface. The 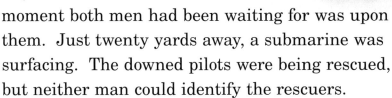 moment both men had been waiting for was upon them. Just twenty yards away, a submarine was surfacing. The downed pilots were being rescued, but neither man could identify the rescuers.

Breathless at the sight of a sub rising through the waves, Dawson and Mueller watched and waited. When the coning tower of the submarine cleared the water's surface, the markings painted on the side boldly identified its origin. Dawson's heart pounded and his stomach churned when he realized it was a German U-boat.

Captain Mueller looked at Dawson and said, "It looks as if I have won our little bet, yes?!"

Water washed from the deck, and saltwater sprayed from the ballast vents of the German submarine. Dawson's heart sank. He knew he was only minutes away from becoming a prisoner-of-war.

Then, Captain Mueller did something most unexpected. Leaning toward Dawson, Mueller whispered, "Captain, you must lay still on the bottom of the raft."

Unsure of what Mueller was doing, Captain Dawson assumed it was a part of taking him prisoner. Reluctantly, he obeyed. The English pilot lay in the bottom of the raft, motionless.

With a hollow metal clank, a hatch on the U-boat opened. Through the small doorway, a group of German sailors and an officer stepped onto the deck and shouted for the attention of the survivors.

Captain Mueller called from the raft to his countrymen standing at the railing of the subma-

German sailors...shouted for the attention of the survivors.

rine. Responding to his request, they threw Mueller a rope and started to pull the raft to the side of the U-boat. While holding onto the line, Mueller pressed his foot against Dawson's chest forcing him to lay still in the bottom of the raft.

The motion of the raft being pulled through the water and the tension of the moment caused Dawson's head to pound. When the rubber life raft reached the side of the U-boat, Captain Mueller shouted to the officer standing on the deck of the submarine. Dawson listened, but was unable to understand the conversation between the two Germans.

Captain Mueller climbed from the raft to the deck of the German sub. The Luftwaffe pilot and the ship's officer continued their discussion.

"What about the British pilot?" the submarine officer asked.

"Forget him," replied Captain Mueller. "He was practically dead when I pulled him from the water and is even worse now. He's not worth our time. Leave him to the sea."

"Yes sir," the German naval officer replied, and then ordered the rest of the sailors back through the hatch and into the submarine. While

the U-boat officer motioned for the rescued pilot
to follow him below deck, Captain Mueller reached
over to untie the raft from the sub. Now that
Dawson realized Mueller's plan was to let him go,
he was more than willing to play dead in the
bottom of the raft.

    Before Captain Mueller pushed the life raft
away from the submarine,
he whispered to Dawson,
"The air and sea have
been most cruel to us.
Next time we meet, let us
hope it will be on land
where we can shake hands."

    With that, Mueller set the rubber raft adrift.
As the raft washed away from the U-boat, Captain
Dawson lifted his head slightly above the side.
He watched the German pilot climb through the
hatch and close it behind him. Moments later, the
sleek black submarine gently slipped beneath the
ocean waves.

    Captain Dawson was alone in the life raft.
Amazingly, the German pilot had not only saved
his life, but spared him from being taken prisoner.
Floating in the choppy water, Dawson wondered if

81

the silk scarf, the one he used to bandage the German's burned hands, had helped secure his freedom.

Although thankful to have avoided capture, Captain Dawson knew he was still in danger. Night was coming, and his chances of being rescued were fading with the daylight. If an English ship didn't find him soon, the odds were slim he would live to see tomorrow.

CHAPTER FOURTEEN

THE HOMECOMING

Nighttime had fallen on Hampton County, and darkness shrouded the Winslow house. Behind the black-out shuttered windows, Harry sat in his room thinking of the day's events. He remembered the look on Captain Dawson's face when he handed him the silk scarf his mother made. Harry's heart sank at the thought of the brave RAF pilot stranded in the English Channel, perhaps lost forever.

Then Harry thought of Erin and how worried she was about her father. Remembering when he surprised Erin with the scarf, Harry's thoughts drifted to his mother's ripped wedding dress and the sacrifice she made. He desperately wanted to help his friends, but felt helpless. The sad situation was making this the worst day of his life.

While Harry sat in his room, he heard a commotion at the front door. Concerned, he started for the stairs to see what was happening. As he made his way to the landing, he overheard his

sister, Susan, explaining something to Mrs. Winslow in a low voice. Susan had brought someone home from the airfield.

Standing at the top of the staircase, Harry couldn't see the mysterious visitor. Wondering who had come to visit at so late an hour, Harry almost fell trying to get a closer look. Halfway down the stairs, he recognized the man standing in the doorway. It was Captain Dawson.

"Captain Dawson!" Harry shouted and threw himself down the remaining steps into the arms of his beloved RAF pilot.

"Careful, Harry," Dawson gently requested, "I'm still a little groggy from floating in a life raft for twelve hours."

Harry looked up at Captain Dawson's face. A bandage was wrapped around the pilot's head, and he seemed pale and weak from his ordeal. Together, all three Winslows, Harry, Susan and their mother helped Dawson into the living room to sit by the warm fire.

"How did you get back?" Harry asked.

In a tired voice, Captain Dawson explained how he bailed out of his crippled Hurricane and ended up in a raft with a German pilot. Astonished, the Winslows stared at each other. Then, Dawson told them how the Luftwaffe pilot saved his life and set him free.

Dawson cocked his head. His own words reminded him of his strange dream, the one he told Simms about in their quarters before breakfast.

"It was like... a dream," Dawson mumbled. "He had me by the throat, but then he let me go."

Harry swallowed hard and thought of his own nightmare.

Dawson continued, "After the German submarine left with Captain Mueller, a fishing boat rescued me. Oddly enough, while I was on board, I couldn't help but notice there was no room for fish. Instead, the ship was filled with radio and radar equipment. It had to be a spy ship from British Intelligence. When we got to port, there was a car with a driver waiting to bring me back to Hampton. Surprisingly, he already knew the way."

Harry, Susan and Mrs. Winslow looked at each other, mesmerized by the story. Although it could have been coincidence, Harry was sure his father was somehow responsible for rescuing Captain Dawson from the English Channel.

"Sadly, Mrs. Winslow, I ruined the beautiful scarf you made for me," Dawson apologized. "But using it to bandage the German pilot's hands may have helped to save me from a German prison camp."

Mrs. Winslow was breathless. "I'm just happy to know my small gift helped, Captain."

Then Captain Dawson turned to Harry.

"When we got back to Hampton, the driver asked to use a telephone. So I took him to Colonel Harrison's office. That's where I ran into Susan.

86

She told me about the call you and Colonel Harrison made to your father. I asked her if she would bring me here so I could personally thank you for saving me."

Confused, Harry stared at Dawson. "But Captain, the German pilot saved you from drowning. Mother's scarf saved you from being taken prisoner. And it must have been father who sent the boat to pick you up. I didn't do anything."

Captain Dawson looked deep into Harry's eyes and tried to explain, "Sometimes, the smallest act of kindness can be the most important. What you do to help doesn't matter as much as that you choose to help. You were ready and willing to do what you could. As it turns out, your actions made the difference. I know your mother made the scarf and your father sent a ship for me, but those things wouldn't have happened without you. Harry, your help combined with the others is what saved my life."

Just as Dawson finished, there was a knock at the front door. When Mrs. Winslow answered, she was glad to see it was Erin. Concerned about Erin and her family, she reached for the ten year old's hand and invited her inside.

"Erin dear, please come in."

Erin stepped through the door and ran to hug Harry. After letting him go, she announced, "A man from British Intelligence just rang up our house. He told us my father is alive and well. You were right, Harry. He was separated from his unit for a couple days, but made it back. Father's coming home soon!"

"That's great news, Erin," Harry replied, happy for his friend.

Mrs. Winslow agreed, "Yes, Erin, come and tell us all about it."

Erin joined the Winslows and Captain Dawson gathered around the fire. She explained how her father had been missing for days. It worried her mother tremendously, and they both feared the worst. The telephone call confirming her father's safety couldn't have been more timely.

"Odd, though," Erin mumbled, "when I answered the telephone, the man on the line knew my name."

Erin breathed a heavy sigh and confessed, "It was horrible not knowing where father was. I had all but given up hope when Harry gave me his beautiful scarf. It reminded me I have friends to help me through bad times. I just wanted to say thanks, Harry."

Harry smiled, a little embarrassed by the attention from Erin. He had no idea the small gift meant so much to her. And yet, for Erin, it seemed to make all the difference.

Glad to be together, the Winslows and their guests continued chatting in the living room for some time. Then, the happy moment was interrupted by another knock at the door. Mrs. Winslow got up to answer, but before she could, a man stepped through the doorway and let himself into the house. Susan, Harry and Erin were speechless. Mrs. Winslow stood frozen, unable to move at the sight of the man standing in her home.

Captain Dawson recognized the stranger as the driver who had brought him back to Hampton. But Harry and Susan, and especially Mrs. Winslow, knew him as someone far more important. The man standing in the doorway was Trevor Winslow. Harry's father had come home.

"Happy Anniversary, dear," Mr. Winslow quietly greeted his wife. Tears of joy started to

pour down Mrs. Winslow's cheeks as she raced to embrace her husband. For the first time in almost two years she was able to hug him on their wedding anniversary.

Somehow, Mr. Winslow had accomplished everything Harry had asked. After making sure that Captain Dawson was rescued, Trevor Winslow, himself, drove the pilot back to Hampton. From Colonel Harrison's office he was the one who called Erin's mother to tell her Mr. Bentley had been found. And best of all, he was able to come home to be with his family when they needed him.

A surprised and excited Harry called to his father, "I thought you said you wouldn't be able to take care of everything."

Mr. Winslow looked at Harry and explained, "I told Mr. Churchill about your telephone call, and he said he could sacrifice a few days without me. So it turns out that I was able to take care of everything, this time. I'm just glad you helped remind me what was important."

Thinking about the rescue of Captain Dawson and Erin's father, Harry began to understand the importance of just being willing to help. As it turned out, no one person was responsible for saving the men. It was only through the combined efforts of many people that Dawson was returned to Hampton, and Erin learned her father was safe. Harry realized that when enough people make a sacrifice and choose to help, anything can be accomplished.

Together, Mr. and Mrs. Winslow walked over to join Harry, Erin, Susan and Captain Dawson sitting around the warm fireplace. The stories they told were filled with happiness, even though the world was at war. The Winslows and their friends knew something special that gave them hope. They lived their lives knowing that when people are willing to help each other, things work out in the end. Harry would never again forget his parent's anniversary. On what almost became the worst day of his life, he learned that helping others was the one way to shed light in the darkest of times.

IN HINDSIGHT

During World War I, combat pilots endured incredible hardships. Not only did they face extreme conditions and danger from enemy planes, many pilots were left no escape if their plane was crippled by combat. Parachutes small enough to fit inside the cockpit were not invented until late in the war. Resulting pilot shortages proved the only thing more important than airplanes are trained airmen to fly them.

After the experience of World War I, military air services like Britain's Royal Air Force recognized the need for improvements in pilot safety. Unlike their unprotected predecessors, World War II RAF pilots were issued parachutes, life preservers, and in some cases small inflatable life rafts. In addition, they were trained to jump clear of damaged planes and use their parachutes and safety gear to survive.

In order to retrieve downed pilots, the RAF developed a simple rescue service. However, the growing number of men needing rescue from the English Channel and North Atlantic Ocean during the Battle of Britain, required the Air Ministry

A pilot parachutes to safety.

to quickly expand their search and rescue system.

The new, highly organized Air Sea Rescue Service divided the British Isles into four regions. Each zone, headed by a group of senior officers was responsible for initiating a sea search at a moment's notice.

Upon receipt of a "Mayday" or "SOS" call, the Air Sea Rescue Service would dispatch an airplane to search and report on the position of the downed pilot or airmen. Then, a high speed motor launch was sent to pick up the survivors. If possible, the search plane would watch over the area until the boat arrived.

Reports of downed men could come from the pilot himself, another pilot, the Coast Guard, Coast Watchers or Royal Observer Corps. In some cases, the local police or general public living in the area would call to inform the service of needed rescue. In order to retrieve survivors, the Air Sea Rescue Service used the RAF Fighter, Bomber, and Coastal Command, as well as the Royal Navy. In addition, Air Sea Rescue also relied on the Royal National Lifeboat Institution, and members of the merchant and fishing fleets located all along the coast of England. Anything that could fly or float carried some degree of responsibility for search and rescue.

Outdated aircraft like Westland Lysanders were typically used in off-shore aerial searches for downed pilots.

Equipped with life raft and sea markers attached to their undercarriage, the short-field take off and landing capabilities of the Lysander proved useful in coastal rescue operations. For searches farther from the coast, medium range Avro Anson and Lockheed Hudson aircraft were dispatched. Primarily used for long range patrols in the North Atlantic, the Short Sunderland flying boat hunted submarines, protected convoys, and rescued survivors of torpedoed ships far out at sea. The Sunderland's range and size made it the ideal search and rescue plane for vast stretches of open ocean.

Short Sunderlands rescued survivors from the North Atlantic.

Although aircraft proved most effective at finding pilots downed at sea, boats were most often used to retrieve them. Specialized rescue launches used by Coastal Command were fast and well equipped. After an air search determined the position of a survivor, a motor launch could race to the area and pick him up. In the event a launch was unavailable, the Air Sea Rescue Service called on local merchant and fishing boats to retrieve pilots as well.

In all air-sea rescue operations, time is critical.

Retrieving survivors from a float.

Low water temperatures surrounding the English coast could prove fatal depending on the time of year. Recognizing the danger of survivors succumbing to the effects of hypothermia, the Air Sea Rescue Service developed an elaborate system of large floats, similar in design to a houseboat. Survivors could swim to the float and climb inside. Painted with brilliant red and yellow banding and Red Cross markings to make them easy to spot, the floats were equipped with radio, food, dry clothing, bunks, and first aid supplies. Outside, a flag was raised to alert patrolling aircraft or surface vessels to the presence of a survivor. Anchored at strategic positions offshore, floats dotted the English Channel from the straights of Dover up to the North Sea.

An ironic compliment to the RAF's Air Sea Rescue Service and their dedication to saving lives, the German

Luftwaffe realized the value of floating rescue stations. They attempted to run a similar rescue scheme. However, the German system was smaller in scale and less efficient. Rescue vessels from both sides often found German airmen inside a British float and RAF pilots in German floats. In each case, the survivors were made prisoners-of-war.

GLOSSARY

Air Vice Marshall: A high ranking officer, second only to Air Marshall.

Ballast Vent: Vents for channeling water used as ballast in submarines.

Captain: A military officer ranking below colonel and above lieutenant.

Coastal Command: A branch of the RAF similar to the Coast Guard

Colonel: A military officer ranking below general and above captain.

Conning Tower: The raised control and observation post of a submarine.

Hardstand: A hard surfaced area next to an airstrip used for parking planes and ground vehicles.

Hawker Hurricane: A type of British fighter plane.

Hedgerow: A row of bushes or small trees that form a fence.

Intercept: To stop or interrupt the progress of enemy aircraft.

Jink Away: RAF term for a sudden evasive action or maneuver.

Junkers Ju 87: A German two-seat dive bomber (also Stuka).

Lieutenant: A military officer ranking below captain.

Messerschmitt 109: A type of German fighter plane (also Me 109).

Operations Building: The airfield's central administration building.

Prime Minister: The head of the English government.

Quick Squirt: RAF term for a short burst of gunfire.

Ropey: RAF term describing something in an uncomplimentary way.

Scramble: The immediate launch of airplanes from the airfield.

Stick or Yoke: The control stick of an airplane used for steering.

Supermarine Spitfire: A type of British fighter plane (also Spit).

U-boat: Term for a German submarine.